W9-ALV-520

DISCARD

HAT TRICKS

Published by
PEACHTREE PUBLISHING COMPANY INC.
1700 Chattahoochee Avenue
Atlanta, Georgia 30318-2112
www.peachtree-online.com

First published in Great Britain in 2019 by Scallywag Press Ltd
10 Sutherland Row, London SW1V 4JT
First United States version published in 2020 by Peachtree Publishing Company Inc.

The illustrations were created with pen, ink, watercolor, and gouache.
Printed in August 2019 by in Malaysia
10 9 8 7 6 5 4 3 2 1
First Edition

HC ISBN: 978-1-68263-150-8

Library of Congress Cataloging-in-Publication Data

Names: Kitamura, Satoshi, author, illustrator.
Title: Hat tricks / written and illustrated by Satoshi Kitamura.
Description: First edition. | Atlanta, Georgia : Peachtree Publishing Company Inc., 2020. |
Summary: A rabbit in a hat performs a magic show. | "First published in Great Britain in 2019 by Scallywag Press"—Copyright page.
Identifiers: LCCN 2019019042 | ISBN 9781682631508
Subjects: | CYAC: Magicians—Fiction. | Magic tricks—Fiction. | Rabbits—Fiction. | Animals—Fiction.
Classification: LCC PZ7.K6712 Hat 2020 | DDC [E]—dc23
LC record available at *https://lccn.loc.gov/2019019042*

HAT TRICKS

Satoshi Kitamura

PEACHTREE
ATLANTA

What do we have here?

It's a **rabbit** in a **hat**!

But it's not just *any* rabbit,
and it's not just *any* hat . . .

It's Hattie the Magician
and this is *her* hat!

So welcome, everyone,
to Hattie's magic show!

Let's say the magic words with Hattie!

Abracadabra, katakurico...

What's in the hat?

It’s a cat!

What will be next?

Abracadabra, katakurico...

What's in the hat?

It’s a squirrel!

Abracadabra, katakurico...
What's in the hat?

It’s an octopus!

Abracadabra, katakurico…

What’s in the hat?

It's a moose!

Abracadabra, katakurico...
What's in the hat?

Why, it's an elephant!

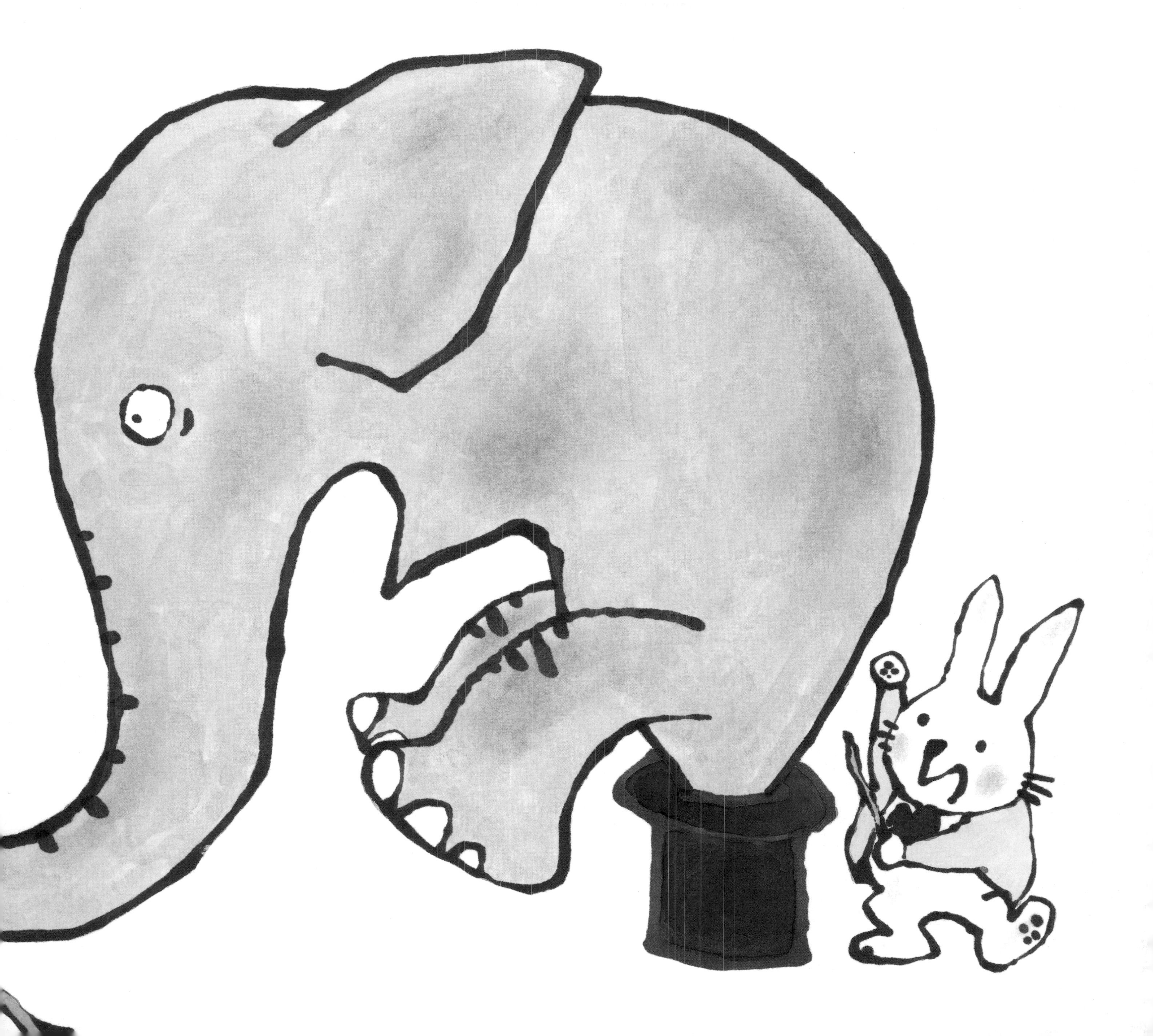

But the elephant is stuck.
Oh, oh, oh, it hurts!

One,
two,
three,
heave,

and…

Kaboom!

All

fall

down!

Well, now the hat
must be empty.
Is it?

WoW!

It’s a whole new world
of friends!

What a *grand finale*.

Brava, Hattie!
Bravo, hat!